TWO BAD PILGRIMS

BY **Kathryn Lasky** ILLUSTRATED BY **John Manders**

Color work by Vince Dorse

VIKING

VIKING

Published by Penguin Group

Penguin Young Readers Group, 345 Hudson Street, New York, New York 10014, U.S.A.

Penguin Group (Canada), 90 Eglinton Avenue East, Suite 700, Toronto, Ontario, Canada M4P 2Y3

(a division of Pearson Penguin Canada Inc.)

Penguin Books Ltd, 80 Strand, London WC2R 0RL, England

Penguin Ireland, 25 St Stephen's Green, Dublin 2, Ireland (a division of Penguin Books Ltd)

Penguin Group (Australia), 250 Camberwell Road, Camberwell, Victoria 3124, Australia

(a division of Pearson Australia Group Pty Ltd)

Penguin Books India Pvt Ltd, 11 Community Centre, Panchsheel Park, New Delhi – 110 017, India

Penguin Group (NZ), 67 Apollo Drive, Rosedale, North Shore 0632, New Zealand

(a division of Pearson New Zealand Ltd)

Penguin Books (South Africa) (Pty) Ltd, 24 Sturdee Avenue, Rosebank, Johannesburg 2196, South Africa

Penguin Books Ltd, Registered Offices: 80 Strand, London WC2R 0RL, England

First published in 2009 by Viking, a division of Penguin Young Readers Group

1   3   5   7   9   10   8   6   4   2

Text copyright © Kathryn Lasky, 2009

Illustrations copyright © John Manders, 2009

LIBRARY OF CONGRESS CATALOGING-IN-PUBLICATION DATA

Lasky, Kathryn.

Two bad pilgrims / by Kathryn Lasky ; illustrated by John Manders.

p. cm.

Summary: Brothers Francis and Johnny Billington take issue with history's account of their troublemaking ways aboard the Mayflower
and in the New World, as they tell their side of the story to Standish Brewster, professor of Pilgrimology at Plimouth University.

ISBN 978-0-670-06168-6 (hardcover)

1. Billington, John—Juvenile fiction. 2. Billington, Francis, ca. 1606–1684—Juvenile fiction. [1. Billington, John—Fiction.

2. Billington, Francis, ca. 1606–1684—Fiction. 3. Pilgrims (New Plymouth Colony)—Fiction. 4. Humorous stories.] I. Manders, John, ill. II. Title.

PZ7.L3274Ty 2009

[Fic]—dc22

2008037645

Manufactured in China   Set in Caslon Antique, Anime Ace, and Harrington   Book design by Jim Hoover

GRATEFUL THANKS TO:

Eric I. Manders & John Morris
The Company of Military Historians
www.military-historians.org

Carolyn Travers, Research Dept.
Plimouth Plantation—www.plimoth.org

Several different kinds of people were onboard the *Mayflower*. At that time, two groups were frustrated with the Church of England, the Puritans and the separatists. The Puritans wanted to "purify" the Church of England. This didn't mean scrubbing the church floors. They intended to make the prayers and the church service simpler and not so fancy. Separatists wanted to separate from the Church of England entirely, and start over in a new land. Other people, like the Billingtons, left England not for religious reasons but for adventure. The separatists were sometimes called Saints, and the pilgrims who came for non-religious reasons were called Strangers. Together, the Saints and Strangers were all called Pilgrims when they left for America.

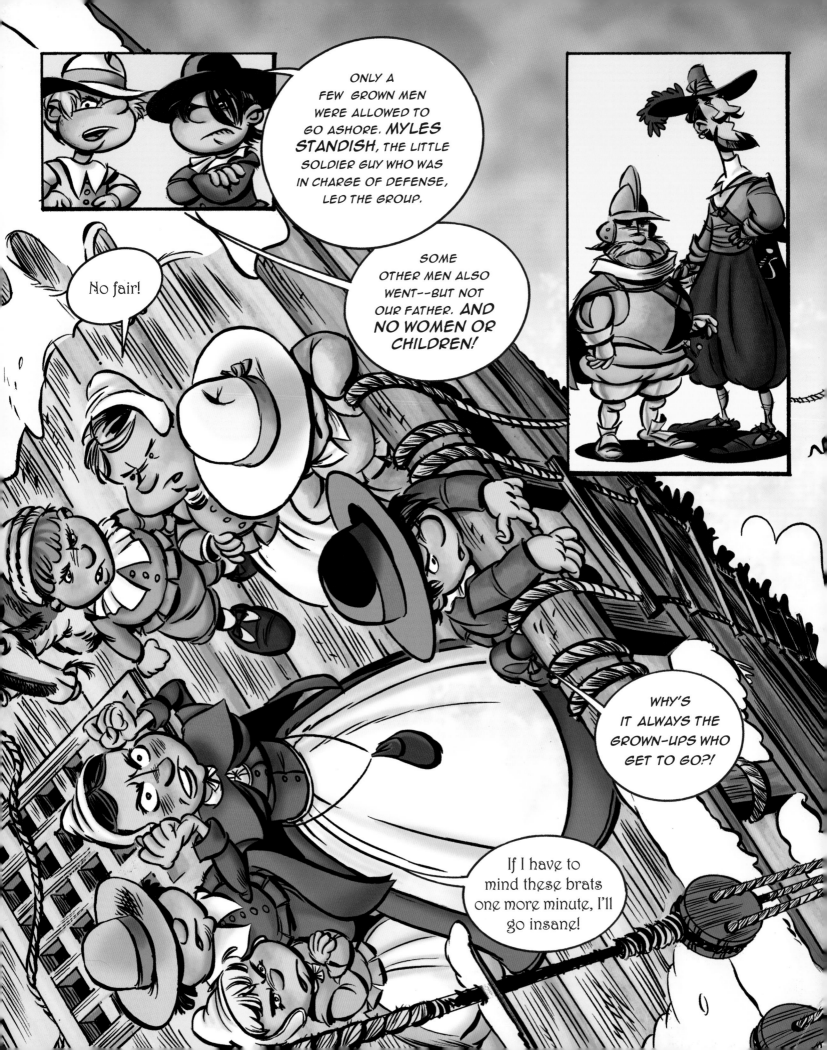

Chapter Three: Great Explorations

The men went ashore to explore and gather wood for cooking. They encountered no signs of people or dwellings and returned to the ship. The following day was the Sabbath.

Though the Pilgrims lost the Indians, they found many things of interest, including a large kettle and several ears of Indian corn buried in holes. They took the kettle and filled it to the brim with corn.

If someone hadn't caught the boys, the squibs could have lit a keg of gunpowder and blown up the whole ship. After this disaster was averted, the Pilgrims thought that they were very special and that God was looking after them. One Pilgrim wrote, "We, through God's mercy, escaped a great danger by the foolishness of a boy, one of Billington's sons, who, in his father's absence, had got gunpowder and . . . made squibs."

Within a short time, the Pilgrims began to move some of their belongings to the first building, which they called the Common House.

On December 28, allotments of land were measured off for each family's home. Bigger families got wider lots. But the weather was stormy, and even though the houses were simple, building took several weeks.

A week later, Francis hiked several miles inland with a grownup to discover two very large lakes. These lakes together became known as the Billington Sea, and still are today.

I WENT, TOO! I WAS THERE! I'M NOT GOING TO LET THEM WRITE ME OUT OF HISTORY.

Imagine naming something after a Billington!

Oh, this is a savage land.

I want to name a big city after me!

Be quiet, Boston.

That same winter, many illnesses struck the company of Pilgrims. Together, they were called the Great Sickness. Entire families were wiped out. But not the Billingtons! They were the only family that escaped without a single loss of life or even one sick day.

Samoset stayed for several hours. They were out of beer, but gave him biscuits, cheese, and pudding. He spoke some English and told them that he had learned it from English fishermen off the coast of Maine, where he came from. The Pilgrim elders were nervous, fearful that he would steal from them.

Chapter Eight: Lost!

But there was no Johnny for almost a month. Finally, the pilgrims heard through Massasoit about a wandering boy who was now living with the Nauset Indians near Cape Cod. These were the very same Indians who had attacked the Pilgrims back on First Encounter Beach. And they were the ones whose corn the Pilgrims had "found" and walked off with. With two Indian guides, the Pilgrims set out to rescue Johnny. They gave the Nauset presents and paid them back for the stolen corn. When they got Johnny back, it turned out the Nauset had loved him. They'd made a huge fuss over him!

Author's Note

Several years ago, I wrote a book about the Pilgrims, their voyage across the Atlantic on the *Mayflower*, and the first ten months of their settlement in Plimouth, Massachusetts. Two of my favorite characters in that book were minor ones, but they were not fictional. Johnny and Francis Billington, along with their parents, Elinor and John, were on the passenger list of the *Mayflower*. The entire family was known for using foul language and for their generally poor behavior. James Deetz, a distinguished colonial historian, called the Billingtons "reckless and turbulent." William Bradford, the first governor of the Plimouth colony, called them "one of the profanest families" to come to the colony. To me, the Billingtons represented an untold aspect of the Pilgrim experience, and I have always wanted to give these two boys a chance to tell their side of the story.

For the purposes of this book, I have taken a bit of poetic license with these real-life rascals. In 1620, Francis and Johnny were ages fourteen and sixteen, slightly older than I have portrayed them here—so they should have known better! But interestingly, in all the accounts written by passengers on the *Mayflower*, the two brothers were referred to as "boys" and sometimes "children," although in that era, boys their age were usually considered adults.

What is absolutely true is that Johnny and Francis were two real Pilgrims who almost blew up the *Mayflower* by experimenting with squibs, as muskets lighters were called. Francis really did discover the lakes that are still known today as Billington Sea and Little Pond. And Johnny really did get lost, living with the Nauset for about a month before the Pilgrims found him, with the help of Massasoit.

And the Billington family's adventures didn't end there. Johnny and Francis's father went on to become the first colonist convicted of murder in America, and was hanged in September of 1630. Six years later, Elinor Billington was put in the stocks and whipped for slandering a neighbor. What a family!

I hope Francis and Johnny's story will help you see that history is not always as black-and-white as it can sometimes appear. Every era has its share of goody-goodies and troublemakers. And I like to think that, as Americans, there's a little Billington in all of us.